Landing in Andonia

A Novelette by Philip Anderson

RED MARE
PRESS

LANDING IN ANDONIA

Edited by Courtney Harler.

Cover design by Emelie Mano.

Interior design by Julianne Johnson.

Author photo by Rory Hamovit.

Art Attribution:
Los Angeles County Museum of Art
A Bear Fighting a Tiger / Series: Battling Animals, pl. 12
Hendrik Hondius I (Flanders, Duffel, 1573–1650)
Antonio Tempesta (after) (Italy, Florence, 1555–1630)
Holland, 1610 / Prints; etching

Red Mare Press / Discover New Art, LLC
70 SW Century Drive, Suite 100442, Bend, Oregon 97702

www.redmarepress.com

Red Mare Press is a division of Discover New Art, LLC. The Red Mare Press name and logo are trademarks of Discover New Art, LLC. The publisher is not responsible for websites (or their content) that are not owned by the publisher.

ISBN 979-8-9901838-3-4

Printed in the United States of America.

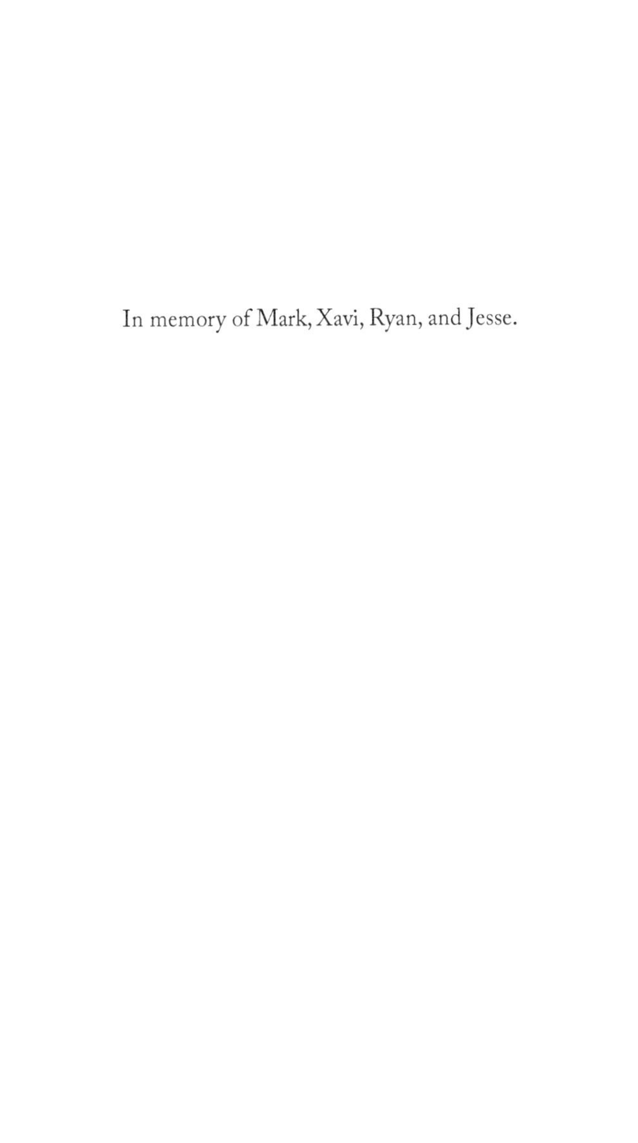

In memory of Mark, Xavi, Ryan, and Jesse.

Foreword

Philip Anderson's *Landing in Andonia* opens with a made-up quotation so convincingly described it requires an internet search to verify it is not true, though the insistence of the premise—that everyone knows the phrase "landing in Andonia"—is, of course, inherently destabilizing: the reader has not in fact heard of it because it is not a real saying that anyone, much less Alexander Graham Bell, has ever said. With this foundation built and destroyed from the get-go, the reader now enters an unsettlingly familiar world, though it also doesn't exist—a more or less middling (in every sense of the word) town called Andonia, allegedly in Illinois, in which all aspects of a middling America are on uncomfortable display, from strip malls and CVS and a "third-tier med school" to a student so overblown with meds and drugs we aren't sure he'll make it to the end of any given sentence, much less his class.

Landing in Andonia's point of view, per its style of deconstruction, is roving—sections are titled (for instance, "The Five-Second Rule Stands in Andonia") and often brief, and may or may not feel fictional in character—a section might comprise a transcript of an interview, or give us characters' unabashed thoughts. The tone throughout is confessional yet acerbic, infected with America's self-medication cocktails of alcohol and prescription meds and ultra-processed foods. There's history here, too, presumably also made up—corrupt politicians, the arcane happenstance that produced a popular honeymoon hotel—and the absurdities both pile up and propel: it isn't clear if the reader is meant to laugh or marvel or wallow in discomfort (seemingly, mostly, the latter). It isn't, in this way, an easy novelette—in its length and structure and tale, it's postmodern plight made anew through its fulsome commitment to it. Anderson's characters themselves are especially pitiable, alternately pathetic and sympathetic, and the complication of how the novelette leaves the reader feeling is where Anderson excels.

In the end, nothing, not Andonia, not America, is really what it seemed at first: even a taxidermied grizzly bear is really a polar bear, dyed brown (with, of course, its own bizarro backstory). And so, Andonia, alleged bellwether of American social mores, is just as hapless, divided, corrupted, and cut off from connection as anywhere else. Via Anderson's acidic sentences and setting we get not just staid or sterile answers but harrowing revelations, as if what's hard about (mostly white) middle America has now been exposed to the morgue's and the narrator's and most of all Philip Anderson's portentous, dissecting light. The dosages of humor, dispersed throughout, are what saves this novelette from being so dark it's just grisly or gratuitous—that, and the reminder of the fabricated narrative of it all. We're a preposterous country with preposterously large, serious, and intractable problems, the story seems to say—woe betide us all. Even if that notion hasn't yet landed in Andonia.

—Hanna Pylväinen

HANNA PYLVÄINEN is the author of *We Sinners*, which received the Whiting Award, and *The End of Drum-Time*, which was a finalist for the National Book Award. Her work has appeared in *Harper's Magazine*, *The New York Times*, *The New York Times Magazine*, the *Chicago Tribune*, and *LitHub*. She is the recipient of fellowships from the Fine Arts Work Center in Provincetown, a Princeton Arts Fellowship at Princeton University, and a Cullman Fellowship at the New York Public Library. She has taught at the University of Michigan, Princeton University, and Virginia Commonwealth University. Currently, she is on the faculty at the Warren Wilson College MFA Program for Writers. She lives in Philadelphia. Find her on Instagram @hannapyl.

1.

Alexander Graham Bell and the Origin of the Saying

In a 1908 interview, Alexander Graham Bell, then head of the Aerial Experiment Association, explained the AEA's hopes for a seaplane developed by Glenn Curtiss. The interviewer asked, "How far can this fly? Can it fly to Chicago? To Andonia?" Bell replied, "It should fly to Andonia, but it won't land in Andonia."[1]

---

1   Gene Smith, "Bell's Man Made Water Bird," *Toronto Daily Star*, November 18, 1908, A6.

2.

Chris Wakes Up from a Nightmare about Jimmy Suggs's Ghost

Chris wakes up from a nightmare about the ghost of Jimmy Suggs. Andonians say Suggs haunts the big cemetery across the two-lane highway from Chris's sad, stucco apartment.

In the dream, Suggs tried to open Chris's car door. Chris was naked. Dr. Grenman was there too. She was naked. He was in a Market Basket parking lot that was both in his hometown in Massachusetts and on the top floor of the med school parking garage. Because dreams know no limits, Chris. Your dreams are unbridled by space and time. Wait, was he having sex with Dr. Grenman in his dream? His boxers are coated.

Chris, you're going to be late for class, you dumbshit, go shower, get up, go.

3.

Lily Sees a Pig-Man at the Only Decent Coffee Shop in Town

Lily's latte is arted, a flower in the foam. She sits at the large live-edge mahogany table. She is pretending to work on her open laptop, but really she's quietly judging everything around her. Next to the table is a seven-foot-tall taxidermied bear that stands with legs spread, arms akimbo, mouth open. Today the bear holds a marker-scrawled poster board sign:

HAPPY 2ND B-DAY FIFTY-FIFTY!

Some zealous barista put a birthday hat on the poor bear because the only decent coffee shop in Andonia is now two years old.

Lily looks past the bear and watches an odd scene unfold on the other side of the plate glass windows. A national news network van is parked outside on Jimmy Suggs Road, and a reporter in a gray suit is interviewing a blue-haired old woman in a purple sweatshirt. On the sweatshirt is a seductively anthropomorphized tabby cat—arm behind head, heavy-lidded eyes, a sly smile, checked hip. The sweatshirt text: *Take a picture, it'll last longer.* The old woman looks dead eyed. She's holding a donut aloft, like she's going to take a bite at any second. The reporter asks the woman something then shoves his microphone toward her. She waves her donut as she answers each question.

This woman is the third Andonian Lily has seen interviewed by some intrepid reporter, and she's only been here for three months.

Lily worries about this old woman when she sees the newsman's cynical smile. The cat sweatshirt is cute but belies naïveté. The newsman is going to twist her words, make whatever she says fit his corporate narrative of the midterm election. Andonia is in a rare swing district that has played a part in the congressional back-and-forth. Currently Andonia has a flamboyantly gay (closeted) and majorly corrupt (obvious) congressman who is facing censure for using taxpayer money to fly his staff and his photographer (boyfriend) to a Taylor Swift concert. No doubt the newsman wants the old lady's opinion on the Taylor Swift concert. Leave this woman and her donut alone, buddy.

Now the interview is interrupted by a large man. *Large* is still an acceptable descriptor of someone that size. He's tall and thick and broad-shouldered. He's got a gut too. Monster truck tire round the middle, really. He looks like a shot-putter, but he is clumsier than any athlete Lily has known. He wants to continue down the sidewalk to the entrance of Fifty-Fifty. He tries to squeeze along the side of the van, but he's wide and graceless. He's got thick pink cheeks, a round face, that rotund middle, and a protruding chest. He looks piggish. Okay, Lily knows she's crossed a line here. *Large* is fine. She can't think of someone as *piggish*. But he is, so she does. He has beady eyes and short-cropped blond hair. Lily *likes* pigs! They're smart! And Lily is a vegetarian. Sometimes. Wow, he really does look like a pig.

Maybe this pig-man is the result of black magic. She can't *earnestly* think that. But maybe. Maybe it's like a fairy tale? A lonely witch tried to transform her pet pig into a human child? Lily knows real Wiccans in San Francisco, so she has an idea about witches. But she pictures this witch as if illustrated in one of Alistair's books. She imagines a watercolored scene: a wooded area, a pen made of broken tree limbs, a smiling green-skinned witch in a pointed hat, and a docile pig beaming up at her as she incants the spell. The pig morphs into this big awkward guy. But the witch dies from exertion before he's a full human! The lost pig-boy wanders the forest uncomfortably upright, tucking his curly tail between his legs.

He definitely still has a curly tail.

Fast-forward to now, and he somehow ends up here in New Balance sneakers, flat-front chinos, and a quarter-zip fleece pullover.

Presently the big clumsy pig-man bumps the old lady being interviewed. She drops her donut. The cameraman pans down to the donut on the ground and pans back up. The woman picks it up, dusts it off, and finally eats it. The large man apologizes, and the lady waves him away. He continues on to the coffee shop. He rushes in and past the bear and Lily's table to the counter. She hears him order a large red-eye coffee and a bacon scone, the cannibal.

4.
Andonia and Vaudeville, A History

Andonia, Illinois, is a synecdoche of Average America, immortalized by a vaudevillian phrase that stems from a bastardization of the *Toronto Daily Star* interview with Alexander Graham Bell, a phrase you have likely heard countless times: "Will it land in Andonia?"

Burlesque great Zeppy Barber explained vaudeville's adoption of the phrase:

> "Will it land in Andonia?" wasn't just about [censoring] sexy and crass things. The people of places like Andonia and Bloomington and Cartersville and Mechanicsburg—it wasn't that they were just religious and proper people, but they had no developed sense of theater. "Will it land in Andonia?" (and the airman screams back, "Not an act for Andonia!") was about anything that didn't fit in the borders of the classic formula. Slapstick

and broad buffoonery and classic soapy drama they liked. Wordplay, satire, parody, *irony*? Not so much.

I once saw Bud [Abbot] and Lou [Costello] do an early version of *Who's on First*—*Who's the Boss* it was then. I saw them do it in Andonia, and I was dying laughing in the wings, but the audience only chuckled at Bud because he was fat and angry and we all know how funny fat-and-angry is. I heard this young guy grumble as he walked out, "The least they coulda done was tell us who the dang boss was!" And the whole crowd around him murmured this fools' agreement: *yeah yeah yeah yeah*.[2]

However, Moira Penfield, a self-published author and tax law professor at Borden College, offers a counterargument in her memoir:

It means we have taste. Andonians have a high bar. If a vaudeville or burlesque act came through town and it was poo-pooed than [sic] that meant

---

2   Paul Lippman, *Vaudeville Follies: An Oral History* (University of California Press, 1971), 161–62.

it wouldn't do well across America. Andonians were the arbiters of mass taste. If it was not an act for Andonia, it was not an act for America. If it couldn't land in Andonia, it wouldn't *fly* anywhere else.[3]

The phrase remains popular and has spawned a trope in news programs: "Will It Land in Andonia?" segments are aired by CNN, Fox, and MSNBC, and they are uniformly two to four minutes of Man-on-the-Street Reporter asks Salt-of-the-Earth Andonians about Hot-Button Issues for Real-American Perspective. Because, as Barber told Paul Lippman, "Andonia is tepid water you don't want to take a bath in, but fine to wash your undies or your dog."[4]

---

3   Moira Penfield, *How I Landed: From Prostitute to Professor, A Memoir of Andonia* (pub. by author, 2011), 3.

4   Lippman, *Vaudeville Follies*, 165.

5.
Chris's Medications

Chris parks his Jeep on the top level of the Illinois University Medical College-Andonia garage. He packs and lights a one-hitter that looks like a half-smoked cigarette. He rolls the window down and lets the November air chill his flushed cheeks and puffy eyes. He hasn't been sleeping, a result of overcaffeination, various prescription drugs, and a penchant for studying late into the night. Still, his standing isn't great, and he fears he's going to fail out of a third-tier med school. He sips his red-eye and wonders why he signed that newsman's release after he tried so hard to not get on camera. He packs his one-hitter again, hits it, and reaches for the bag that had his bacon-cheddar scone in it. He forgot that he ate it on the short drive here, and he worries again about his memory and attention span. He wants to pin it to sleep loss, but it could also be a side effect of the weed. Or the methylphenidate or the clonazepam he's been popping back and forth depending on which he needs, up or down. His heart is racing again. He knows better, he knows better, he knows better about his family history of high blood pressure and cholesterol and heart disease. His father has warned him time and again about his diet, but Chris is his mother's fat son, has her lack of impulse control. He has his maternal grandfather's thick body. That's fine if he's more his mom's family than his dad's because Dad is a bald alcoholic and Chris will never lose his hair. But his father's brother is also a renowned heart surgeon and there's admittedly shame around where Chris ended up for med school, but if he gets through it he'll be fine, his uncle says, he'll set him up, don't worry. But he has to get through it.

Chris reaches into the glove box and grabs the methylphenidate, downs a ten-milligram, a small dose, don't worry, don't worry, don't worry, Chris, your heart will be fine.

6.
Andonia's Industries, Part I: Healthcare

Andonia has two major industries. The second largest is healthcare. Andonia is home to the Illinois University Medical College-Andonia (IUMCA), Borden College (a small liberal arts college with a popular graduate program in healthcare administration), and the Organization of Catholic Hospitals (OCH), a denominational healthcare group that operates hospitals and clinics in Indiana and Illinois, including two hospitals and a nursing college in Andonia. In an effort to give back to the community and to promote health in Andonia, IUMCA and OCH, in partnership with the city's parks department, run a family-friendly, affordable gym and recreation complex along the river called the AndyPlex.

7.
Lily's Quotidian Life

In an empty exercise room in the AndyPlex, Lily practices a modern dance routine she plans to use for audition tapes. She does this every day, part of the schedule: Drop off sister at work. Drop off nephew at preschool. Coffee and app essays at Fifty-Fifty. Rehearsal and shower at AndyPlex. Pick up nephew from preschool, take him home, eat Cheerios, play with trains, prep dinner. Pick up sister from work, come home, make dinner, watch TV, read book, go to bed. The schedule is meant to keep Lily sane and sober. But she indulges on Sundays. She buys orange juice and champagne because her sister loves mimosas. Lily ends up drinking the whole bottle herself, minus a few sips, and her sister drinks most of the orange juice. It's fine, her sister is six months pregnant.

Today Lily's schedule has a detour to the Kroger where she buys acorn squash, zucchini, brown rice pasta, pesto, and tomatoes. She has her nephew seated in the cart. He tends to stay silent around his aunt. He keeps staring over Lily's shoulder as if at someone following them. She turns, and no one is there.

"Do you see someone behind me, Alistair?"

He looks down at the floor, mutters no.

"Do you see a ghost?" she says. "I've seen ghosts. It's okay if you see ghosts because I've seen ghosts."

He rolls his eyes, says, "You're being dumb."

"That's not a nice thing to say to your aunt."

"Ghosts aren't real, and you are dumb."

"Then why is a ghost telling me to do this?" Lily pushes the cart hard and lets it go, and it drifts unmanned down the aisle. She watches with satisfaction as her nephew's face crumples in terror, but jogs and catches the cart before it hits the "ethnic condiments" section—salsa, Sriracha, soy sauce, hot sauce. Asian and Latin clumped together because it is all foreign and indiscernible in Andonia.

"The ghost wants us to buy this," she says to a wailing Alistair as she pulls a bottle of Cholula off the shelf. She adds, "C'mon, don't cry. It was a friendly ghost, I swear."

They drive downtown and idle in front of the large smoked-glass building that takes up a whole city block. This is the home of Howell Industries, where Lily's sister is a lawyer.

"What's for dinner?" Lily's sister asks when she gets in the car.

"Brown rice pasta with tomatoes and zucchini."

"I want Cheerios," Alistair says from his car seat.

"You know I don't want pasta."

"It's brown rice pasta," Lily says. "You won't gain any weight."

"Can we at least do a meat sauce?"

"I thought we were being vegetarians," Lily says. "I got pesto."

"I've got pregnant cravings but yeah, I guess we'll be vegetarians."

"I want Cheerios."

"Cheerios are vegetarian," Lily says.

"I don't care," Alistair says.

Lily says, "You should care, Alistair, because all the animals in the books you love, do you want to eat them?"

"I'll eat the wolf," he says after some consideration. "He ate the pigs, so it's only fair."

8.
Andonia's Industries,
Part II: Howell

Andonia's major industry is large-machinery manufacturing, thanks to Howell and its subsidiaries. Howell Industries has factories in Andonia, East Andonia, and the Andonia suburb, Wendover. Howell is the major employer in Andonia, responsible for nearly forty thousand jobs. James Howell II founded Howell Farming Equipment in 1907. Howell now makes machinery and vehicles for construction, mining, and mass farming. Howell Industries' recognizable blue-and-yellow triangular logo, found on backhoes and beanies alike, has become a symbol of the American workingman as much as Carhartt jackets and Red Wing boots. Howell Industries has a lesser-known subsidiary called JFH Defense that makes combat tanks. The tanks are sold primarily to sub-Saharan African and Middle Eastern nations. In order to distance the JFH Defense department from the wholesome construction equipment, the tanks and defense vehicles are manufactured in factories in

North Carolina, and none of the tanks are stamped with the famous logo. But the engineers of these war machines all live in Andonia, Illinois.

9.
Chris at Home

Chris lives in a stucco three-story Pepto-pink complex with a man-made pond that attracts ducks and mosquitos and smells like sewage when it is not frozen. The complex is off the two-lane highway that runs north-south through the town. The highway is littered with strip malls of repeated chain stores—parking lots surrounded by fast-food restaurants and home-improvement megastores—and smaller, sadder strip malls with drugstores and independent nail and hair salons, dry cleaners, and noodle shops. Chris's stucco complex is behind a strip mall with a Popeyes, CVS, Beauty by Angela, Cigarettes More!, and an Aloha Jim Café, which claims it serves Kona coffee but that shit tastes like it's got chicory in it. Chris has been to New Orleans, he's had the famous beignets. He's been to Kauai, he's windsurfed. He knows the difference between Kona and Café Du Monde. Chris doesn't go to Aloha Jim, he goes to Fifty-Fifty.

But Chris frequents the CVS for his meds, and tonight he stops at Popeyes before heading home to his third-floor apartment. The complex is set up like a cheap motel—no hallways, just exposed doors and railings that look down on the man-made pond and the ducks that fell for it—so Chris can see from the lot that his neighbor Harvey is standing outside his door waiting for him. Chris sucks on his fountain Dr Pepper and takes his time climbing the drafty stairwell, idling on each landing.

"Doc," Harvey calls when Chris makes it to the third floor. He's waving a plastic sandwich bag. "Doc, I gotta show you!"

Chris puts the Dr Pepper and Popeyes on his welcome mat and walks over to Harvey. The old man is thin, wiry, bald, and wears a classic Western costume. The leather vest, the big buckle, the fucking snake-killer boots. He's got a polyester shirt tucked into tight black Levi's, and he's holding up his liver-spotted hand with its turquoise-laden jewelry flashing in the sunset, the sandwich bag flopping in Chris's face.

"Let's see, Harv," Chris says.

He takes the bag and holds it against the dying light of the evening sky. The contents of the sandwich bag are, once again, Harvey's excrement, which was a fun game to play at first, but this fucking guy…. Chris can't keep it up much longer.

"Look, Harv." Chris squeezes the bag a couple times, keeps it held up to the red sunset. He closes one eye like he's examining it for something special. The bag is cold. The old man must have fished this shit out of his toilet a while ago. Or maybe he shat right into the bag. "Look, Harv," he says again, "I can see that what I told you last time is definitely right. No more liquor after six p.m., cut out white bread, and you should really cut back on the cigarettes, my man."

Chris swings the bag near his ear, pantomimes listening, and adds, "Liver, kidney, and intestines are saying to me, 'Save me, Doc, save me!' That's what all that indigestion is about. It's really the drinking, Harv."

"You got all that from that?" Harvey points at the bag.

"Well, it's the fourth sample this week, and I can say conclusively now that you really need to stop drinking, but I get it, that's hard, so at least don't have any after six p.m."

"Why after six?"

"The sun, Harv," Chris says confidently. "Vitamin D!" In truth, Chris wants to stop hearing his neighbor crying through the paper-thin wall that separates their apartments, something that happens like clockwork after Harvey has downed a fifth of Beam during *Wheel of Fortune.* "You gotta drink sleepytime tea and go to bed, maybe as early as nine, and try to sleep until eight, really catch up on all those years of sleep you missed in your wilder days, my man."

In his apartment, Chris eats a fried chicken thigh before he remembers to wash his hands. He takes a milligram of clonazepam and turns on the news, wondering if he'll see himself.

10.
Harvey's Secret, Part I

Harvey Mulligan once beat a man to death with a stool after they had an argument in a bar on the street that is now called Jimmy Suggs Road. The street then was called Smith Street, and the bar where the two men had the fatal argument is still called Smith Street Bar. The old man, then very young, was convicted of involuntary manslaughter. He was sentenced to fifteen years.

11.
Lily at Home

"Tomorrow you have your GTA thing, right?" Lily's sister asks. "Because I was thinking I'll take the car tomorrow. Secretary on my floor, she's back from her maternity leave—they just give a fucking month—"

"Well," Lily says. Because she has already expressed time and again that she can't believe her sister left DC to be a corporate shill in this hellhole. But her sister wanted a job she could leave at five every day, especially with a second kid on the way.

Lily's real problem is with her sister's husband who encouraged the move, then kept his government contract. He's in DC alone for another three months. "Call Lily," the husband suggested to Lily's sister when he told her about his contract extension. He is Australian and talks with an annoying upspeak inflection. "Get Lily to help with *Alastair*. Her life's a *shemozzle*. She doesn't have a *real job*. She's living at *your mum's*. She should get out of San Francisco after *going troppo*. It'll be good for you *and her*."

"Well, yeah, fuck Howell, this is temporary." Lily's sister has explained this all before. She took the DC firm job out of law school, billed seventy hours a week and put the parental burden on her husband. When she got pregnant the second time, she hunted down in-house jobs, and Howell was the first one to make an offer. She took it, but she only plans to be here for another year. "I'm not raising my children here," she told Lily the first week she was in Andonia.

"What the fuck was I saying? I swear to god, fucking pregnant brain."

"You want to take the car," Lily says. "Because a secretary had a baby?"

"Christening," she says. "The secretary is having a christening tomorrow night at some church and invited me and Alistair. So I can leave work early, pick him up from preschool, and then we can go to the christening of Hunter or Colton or whatever this kid's name is, and you don't have to taxi us around. And since tomorrow you're doing that GTA thing, right?"

"Right."

"I can drop you off at the med school in the morning and you can take a cab home later."

"You can drop me at Fifty-Fifty," Lily says, "I'm not doing the GTA thing until the afternoon and I can walk to the med school from there."

12.
Churches

Andonia has more than three hundred Christian churches. It has two Jewish temples, one Unitarian Universalist church, and one mosque.

There is a historical plaque outside St. Anthony's Garden Cemetery to mark where the first and last Visionist churches were built then burned.

13.

Chris Sees the Pretty Girl at the Only Decent Coffee Shop in Town

Chris is at the mahogany table next to the taxidermied bear, books and laptop spread out in front of him. The girl with the long straight hair and the sleeve of floral tattoos puts her bag down at the other end of the table. She asks him to watch her stuff while she gets her coffee.

"Sure thing," he says.

"What are you working on?" he asks her after they've sat at the table for an hour in silence. She keeps looking at him, he can see it out of the corner of his eye. But she's so pretty he's been afraid to look back. She's probably not interested but whatever, it's worth a shot, Chris. "What are you working on?" he asks again after she takes her earbuds out, says, "Hm?"

Both their mugs are empty. Both have plates with just crumbs. He's become what he hates, what his father really hates: people who take up space. But he's got exams later and he's gotta cram, and he feels at ease with taking up space when he's talking to the pretty girl.

"I'm going over some stuff," she says. "I'm teaching something later and I need to make sure I have all the materials down."

"Oh cool," he says. She's staring at him. Why is she staring at him. "What do you teach?"

"Usually dancing, but today is something different."

"I got two left feet," he says. Now's the kicker. "Maybe you could teach me to dance sometime?"

"Maybe," she says. She said it high-pitched, bad sign. High-pitched means probably not. Low and silky means skip the dancing, let's fuck. But she said "maybe" high-pitched, Chris.

He turns back to his books, defeated. The blood drains from his face.

"What are *you* working on?" she asks.

Is she interested, why is she carrying on the conversation?

"I'm a comedian," he says. Chris points to his open medical textbooks. He holds up *Gross Anatomy*. "Right now I'm working on my tight five. I wanna make sure my jokes are scientifically sound."

"Oh," she says. "Is that sarcasm?"

"Sorry, yeah," he says. "A joke about jokes. That's me."

Chris no longer feels okay about taking up space. Pack up your bags and leave, Chris.

"I have to get going," he tells her. He's standing at the taxidermied bear. The birthday hat is still on the poor thing. He fears she is comparing their sizes.

"Nice talking to you," she says. She leaves her mouth open and stares up at him. An ellipsis and a question mark on her face.

"Chris."

"Nice talking to you, Chris," she says. "I'm Lily."

14.
Andonia's Prodigal Son

Jimmy Suggs Road was named for Jimmy Suggs in 1998. Suggs is the most celebrated Andonian, with his storied stand-up career and his series of comic-caper films. The renaming of Smith Street to Jimmy Suggs Road was not without controversy, however. Many religious organizations objected to the honor because of Suggs's famous stand-up routines decrying God and espousing atheistic beliefs. They also found his ironic portrayal of God in the Heaven Sent film series to be blasphemous. The *Catholic Times* once called Suggs's comedy "hedonistic"[5] in response to Suggs's famous set likening God to an abusive, beer-swilling 1950s-era deadbeat dad who was upset his only son grew his hair out, wore flowy robes and sandals, and spent a lot of time talking about Free Love. ("To think I set that queer up with a great job as a carpenter!") Suggs's own father worked the line in the Howell factory in East

---

5   Stephen McCarthy, "Missing His Father's Love," *Catholic Times*, January 11, 1987, B6.

Andonia and died of cirrhosis of the liver when Jimmy was seventeen years old.

Suggs, while Andonia's most famous son, was not a fan of his hometown, and requested in his suicide note that he be buried in Los Angeles.[6] Despite his wishes, his sister had his ashes interred in a family tomb in St. Anthony's Garden Cemetery.

6   Tanisha Freeman, "Comedy and Tragedy: The Jimmy Suggs Story," *Atomic Bomb*, August 1995, 21.

15.
Lily Goes to Dr. Grenman's Office

"I'll have the students come in groups of five into the examination room, and only one of each group will actually touch you," Dr. Grenman says.

Dr. Grenman is Lily's sister's neighbor. Lily met Dr. Grenman at a barbecue. She told her about her time as a GTA in San Francisco. Dr. Grenman, a tall woman with a warbly voice and a Midwestern accent, suggested Lily volunteer at the medical school.

Here at the school, Lily sees Dr. Grenman's face is all business, and her dark brown hair, parted on the side, comes down to just beneath her ears. She wears pearl earrings and wire-framed glasses, a blue blazer and a pumpkin blouse. She reminds Lily of a US senator.

"As it is your body," Dr. Grenman says as they walk the wide hallway to the examination room, "you will choose the students who will give you the exam."

Lily was trained as a GTA—Gynecological Teaching Assistant—at UCSF, a position she volunteered for after an ob-gyn told her she would not have gotten gonorrhea if she had been less promiscuous. At UCSF she sat in an examination room and told second-year med students about scenarios they might see, about the variety of female-bodied people who could be their patients, and about the different levels of comfort or discomfort these women or trans men or nonbinary patients feel with strange hands on their bodies. Lily had practiced her speech on her walk here. "This is about bedside manner, this is about professionalism, this is about respect. If my legs are spread and a doctor tells me in a singsongy voice that *I wouldn't have the clap if I better knew the men I took home* then that doctor is not someone I want touching my body."

The teaching examination room at IUMCA where Lily sits in a paper gown is larger than an average exam room in a typical doctor's office. Five plastic chairs and one rolly desk chair line the wall by the door.

The first few groups are fine, except for small hiccups. In one, a young man said, "I'm going to pull out now," at which point Dr. Grenman said, "Tell her what she'll feel, not what your actions will be."

"Also, *pulling out* is poor phrasing," Lily added.

The last group of five students enters, and Lily is surprised to see Chris bumbling in with pink cheeks and smelling faintly of marijuana.

"Okay," Dr. Grenman says. "This is Lily, and she will be assisting by acting as a real-life patient. We will go over proper conduct and language, and she will read out several scenarios you might encounter. Let's do the first one."

"Doctor," Lily says, "I am saving myself for marriage but my boyfriend and I have been having anal sex, and lately it's been very itchy."

"Okay, who knows what to say here?"

16.
Chris Examines Lily

She's naked in front of him, and she has pointed at him, made him come up to her naked body, touch her breasts, tell her if he feels anything. Of course he feels something, he has feelings or something, but no, not those feelings. She's not asking about feelings. Are there lumps in her mammary glands, does she have cancer? Is the cancer caused by her cell phone? Is the cancer caused by the immoral acts she has committed?

"Okay," he says. "Cancer is not caused by any immorality. No diseases are caused by immorality." He is looking at Dr. Grenman, his hand still on Lily's breast. "Cancer is caused by genetic mutation sometimes onset by exterior factors like UV rays or inhalation of chemicals. Breast cancer, while it can be affected by drugs and smoking and other factors, is likely hereditary, and here it would be appropriate for me to ask about family history of the patient."

"Then go ahead and ask her." Dr. Grenman frowns at him.

"Ma'am—"

"I prefer *miss*," Lily says.

"Miss," he says. "Do you know of anyone in your family who has had cancer?"

"I do not know," Lily says. "I was adopted. My birth mother was a Russian ballerina who defected to the United States while touring. She died in childbirth. The Russian government deny she existed, and I have been unable to locate records of her or of my family history. I only know what I know because this is the story she told the hospital where I was born. My birth father was never identified. You see, I am a genetic orphan."

"Whoa," Chris says. Wait, is this true or the scenario? He should not have smoked before this class. He didn't know this was happening today. He thought exam meant written test. He was not expecting to be touching this girl like this. Oh shit, his hand is still on her boob.

"Well," he says, putting his arms at his side. "I don't feel anything, and as far as your interesting history, if you would like to know about your ancestry there are DNA tests you can take now. They can help you decipher if you're susceptible to any diseases, which can assist your primary care physician when it comes to taking care of your health."

"Have you done the DNA test, Doctor?" Lily asks Chris. She has affected a Russian accent.

"Yeah," he says, "found out I'm four percent Sephardic Jewish."

"Really?" Lily asks.

"Nobody expects the Spanish Inquisition!"

Dr. Grenman unexpectedly guffaws, stops, and shakes her head. She jots a note on a piece of paper, thanks Lily, and dismisses the class except for Chris.

"I can smell the weed on you," she tells him when they're alone. "And your eyes are incredibly bloodshot. Unfortunately, I'm going to have to report this, and with how things are going for you, I don't think it will end well."

Is Chris trembling from fear, from meds, or from the warmth of Lily's breast still on his palm? He stammers out, as best he can, "Okay."

"Not okay," Dr. Grenman says. "Pretty bad, actually. But we'll see what happens."

She takes his arm and walks him to the door.

Lily idles in the hallway. She looks up and smiles, and Chris feels like his heart is going to explode, the fucking Ritalin.

"You want to get a drink?" she says before he can speak. She's leaning coolly against the wall, her sweater draped over her shoulders. "I have the night off and don't know anyone in town. Is there a cocktail bar here?"

Chris remembers hearing about the bar at the newly reopened Hotel Jeanne D'Arc.

"Cool," she says. "You free now?"

17.

The Hotel Jeanne D'Arc and the Visionists, Histories

The Hotel Jeanne D'Arc was built in 1917 with primary investment from James Howell II. The hotel was a grand plaza meant to host Howell's business partners and clients who came to see the famous Howell factories and the engineers who were crafting advanced designs on motorized farm equipment. The Hotel Jeanne D'Arc was named by its architect, the Philadelphian Martin Dufresne, who believed the name should reflect the history of the town.[7] Andonia was first settled by French trappers in the late seventeenth century. The town did not grow until the early nineteenth century when Andonia became what was supposed to be the temporary home of a matriarchal Christian utopian cult called the Visionists. Visionism practiced economic austerity, and it banned men from educational and religious services. Men were instructed to gather on full moons and scream, to reconnect with

---

7   Stephen Wilkinson, "Architect Promises Grand Hotel by River," *Andonia Tribune*, September 21, 1915, 1.

the inner animal. Mater Joan, the leader of Visionism, had visions from God, and these included one wherein she saw that Adam never ate the fruit of knowledge, that knowledge and humanity were particulars of women. Mater Joan's visions allowed her to become a tyrant who sent women she deemed more beautiful than she to work in the fields or in dark basements. Joan made men leave their wives for her. And after seven years, the flock revolted and Visionism disintegrated. Those who revolted, including Joan's sister, burned Joan at the stake as a nod to her namesake.[8] They also burned the churches and all else in the Mater's Community, leaving only the small graveyard. The graveyard has expanded over the years and is still operational as St. Anthony's Garden Cemetery. The rest of the Mater's Community land is now highway, strip malls, and Pepto-pink apartment complexes with man-made ponds.

The luxuriousness of the Hotel Jeanne D'Arc helped promote the city as a cosmopolitan place to come to, and by 1925, Andonia was the most popular honeymoon destination in Illinois. But the hotel went bankrupt two years ago. The couple who owns Fifty-Fifty scored at auction the taxidermied bear that once stood in its lobby. The hotel reopened in

---

8   Lupita Hernandez-Epstein, *Heaven on the Plains: A History of Failed Utopian Societies in Illinois from Andonian Visionists to Zion Doweites* (University of Chicago Press, 2009), 14–65.

September after being bought and refurbished by Minnette Hotels, and it is now officially called The Hotel Jeanne D'Arc, a Minnette Grand Marquee.

18.
Lily's Ghost

She doesn't know why she's attracted to him. He's not bad-looking, he's just a big guy with small-guy energy. Nervous energy. He's combustible, she feels it.

The cocktail menu is long, so she orders a glass of wine. She sits in the half-moon of a banquet bench at a faux-marble table and waits for the pig-man—Chris! *Christ*, Lily, don't call him a pig to his face—to set up a tab.

"What'd you get?" she asks. He's carrying a Marie Antoinette coupe.

"A French 75," he says. "Bartender called it a 'Freedom 76' though."

They talk about Andonia, this odd place in the middle of the country, and he fidgets his fingers, tears his cocktail napkin.

"Actually, Lebanon, Kansas, is the middle of the country," Chris says. "Contiguous forty-eight at least. I looked it up. We're about five hundred miles east of dead center. But that's not that far."

He asks why Lily is in Andonia, and she explains away her sister and Alistair and Australian brother-in-law in a couple sentences. But why is he here? She recognizes an accent, Northeast?

"I'm from Massachusetts," he says.

"I knew it. I went to college in Amherst."

"I'm from North Shore," he says. "Gloucester."

Glawstuh, he says. A port town. Not the magical forest she had first envisioned.

"So why didn't you go to medical school closer to home?"

"This was the only one I got into." His MCAT score was low, he tells her. He was surprised he got in anywhere. "So I 'landed in Andonia' as they say, and now, I dunno…. I guess I'm here."

She finishes her glass of wine, asks him to get her another one. She watches him closely at the bar. He takes out a bottle of pills, and she worries he is trying to roofie her. Instead he pops a pill himself and swallows it dry.

"Viagra?" she asks when he places the wine down.

"Ha, no," he says. His face is hopeful but dubious. "Ritalin, actually."

"Is that why I could feel your heart beating in your fingers earlier?" His hand had been warm and pulsing as he examined her. It was exciting. "Or were you just happy to see me?"

"She's got jokes," he says, but his laugh is forced, sad.

Lily is hitting on him, but she can see he doesn't believe it's real.

She leans into him, flicks her hair. She wants his energy to change. She wants him to know it's real, and she wants him to kiss her. She drinks her wine too eagerly. She wants a gin martini. She wants to leave Andonia. She wants to run off to the forest with him, back to the witch's hut. If there was a witch that could turn Lily into an animal, she would like to be a bird, something soft but strong. A finch. How would a finch and a pig work out?

He leans in now too, puts his face close to hers. If he kisses her, she will get to see him naked. She needs to know if he has a curly tail. Because she wants to know if the world is more than the parts we can see. She wants to prove her mother and sister wrong, but maybe they're right. She wants to know if she really is losing grip on reality.

"Why did you come here," he asks again. "You're too pretty to be here. Too cool. Why did you leave San Francisco?"

"The truth is complicated," she says conspiratorially. "But here it is. I wasn't in San Francisco anymore. I was living at my mom's in Marin. I was working as an after-school dance instructor, getting paid forty dollars a day. The children were brats, and my boss sucked.

She was rarely around, but when she was, she would bully me. She would completely embarrass me in front of these kids by calling me an idiot or saying I was messing up my dance moves, or she was outside on her phone talking to someone in French and smoking cigarettes, and I'd be left alone with the kids for the full two-hour program. She always left at five on the dot whether or not the kids had been picked up, and she would expect me, who was not getting compensated for overtime, to wait until the parents came. That is the base of the problem, and it only gets worse because," she finishes her wine before she finishes her sentence, "then my friend Silvia died."

Chris smiles in a way to let her know she can continue talking, that he is listening, and he will not interrupt her with his own horrid life tale. But that's not enough.

"I'm going to need you to get me a gin martini—dry with a twist—if I'm going to finish this story," she says. He nods and heads to the bar.

She studies the dregs of her wine glass. Why is she trusting him so wholly with her story? There is something magical about him, she is sure.

"I'm sorry about your friend," he says when he returns with her martini.

"It was a drug overdose," Lily continues. "Silvia. She'd been depressed. Her girlfriend broke up with her.

The girlfriend had moved out, leaving Silvia with the full rent. It was, like, a nice one-bedroom in Bernal Heights. The girlfriend was a trust-fund girl with an art job and good drug dealers. She didn't like me. It had created a rift in my friendship. So Silvia was going to have to give up her place, and she had nowhere to stay. Her parents had put her in gay conversion therapy when she was seventeen, so she obviously couldn't go home. And Silvia was kind of a mess before the breakup. She had alienated a lot of friends because, I don't know, she and her girlfriend had just become party monsters and were doing a lot of drugs and hanging out with like, whatever, not the wrong crowd, just like the people who are your temporary friends, you know? When Silvia texted me it was for the first time in months. She said, *haha, long time no talk, anyway, bitch left me and I won't have a home soon haha.* In retrospect, I see she was asking to stay with me and my mom. But I was reading the text while I was at work, and my boss yelled at me like 'Your generation and phones, engage the children, phone away!' so I tossed the phone in my bag, and by the end of the class I'd forgotten to respond. A couple days later," Lily says, "Silvia was found dead on the kitchen floor by a real estate agent who was showing the place."

Silvia's death deepened Lily's own depression, she tells Chris. "I was already a drinker, but I began drinking heavily on weeknights. I was guilty, obviously. I kept thinking, if I had responded to the text, she'd have had a fighting chance. And I drank the guilt away. My job started every day at two p.m., so I could sleep off the hangover and go out after work again."

"It's not my place to say," Chris says, "but it's not your fault."

"Thank you. Yes. And logically I knew it wasn't my fault," Lily says, "but guilt doesn't need logic to thrive, and logic really stepped out the door about a month after Silvia died."

Lily drinks her martini down in a gulp because the story she is about to tell Chris is what got her banished to Andonia.

"Almost a month after she died, Silvia came to me. As a ghost," Lily says. "I was hungover. I went to a movie, a matinee. My mom's town has an art house theater that shows classic films, and I went to see Antonioni's *L'Avventura*. I was sitting in the back of the theater, under the projection room. I could hear the film reel the entire time I was in there, like it was on a loop and clicking, and it had this easy, beautiful rhythm to it. The best way I could put it is I fell into a trance. This is me trying to find logic. I'm in the back of this old, empty theater, listening consciously or not to this rhythmic hum-and-click above my head, and I'm sitting in the dark, alone, with only this sad black-and-white movie. I walked out of the theater without really remembering anything about the movie other than it was sad and it was about a missing girl. I felt I had been hypnotized. So I came out of the theater and I walked along the main road downtown in kind of a daze and I head over to Safeway where I run into my boss.

"'You look absolutely terrible,' my boss said to me. I was standing in front of the premade sushi. This awful woman with her caftan and her expensive sculptural jewelry is looking at me, through me, and she clearly sees I'm in a state and she says *You look absolutely terrible*. Then in the next breath she says, 'I'm so glad I ran into you you need to come in early to clean up before the students get there I tried calling you but it went straight to your message and your voice mailbox is full you should delete your messages.'

"So she sees I'm in a state and starts demanding things of me, and my only response to her is *Okay yes no problem* because I don't know how to stand up to this woman, and then there she was. Silvia was leaning against the fish counter just behind my boss. She was looking at king crab legs and salmon fillets and then she looked up from the counter and said,

"'You should tell this bitch to shut the fuck up.'"

"And did you?" Chris asks.

"No," she says. "I broke down crying. I was a wet, soppy mess on the floor of the grocery store, and my boss said, 'Don't come in today if that's how you're going to act,' then she walked away. Silvia, her ghost, walked up to me, and she said, 'You really should have told that bitch to shut the fuck up.' And I said, 'You're not real. You're dead. This is not real.' I left Safeway, and Silvia—the ghost of Silvia—followed me. She walked with me back to my mom's house. She came with me out to the bar. She told me she knows I'm destined for something. She watched me drink myself into an oblivion. I blacked out and she was gone. I came to at home and my mother was standing over me. Two days later my sister calls, tells me she'll buy me a flight out here. My friend Silvia died and came to me as a ghost, and that's how I landed in Andonia."

"I'm sorry," Chris says. He's fidgeting with the stem of his glass.

"I've been here three months. This is the longest conversation I've had with anyone outside of my sister in three months."

"Now I'm definitely sorry," he says, laughing. "I'm such a waste of conversation."

"You have to stop that," she says. She notices his cocktail napkin is torn into fifty pieces.

"What?"

"Stop with the self-deprecation," she says. "Stop being so small, big guy."

"What?"

She wants him to tell her she is unstable, not that she believes in stability anymore. She no longer lives in a world of reason. She knows there is so much more than what we can see. She knows that from his semi-expert medical standpoint, he would say the ghost wasn't real, that it was a trick of grief, a hallucination of depression. She wants to tell him that he's wrong, that he's blind and she has one eye. The ghost was real, and maybe so was the witch who made him. She gets to live in a world where fairy tales and ghost stories are true. She gets to believe what she wants to believe.

"Let's get out of here," she says. "I like you, and I want to see you naked."

19.
Frank Howell's Penthouse

During World War II, the Hotel Jeanne D'Arc suffered because of a decrease in tourism to Andonia, but Howell Industries, whose engineers expanded the uses of their farm equipment to construction and defense vehicles in order to support the war effort, soon became a titan. James Howell II's son, James Francis Howell III (better known as "Frank"), was a decorated Army Air Force pilot and the most eligible bachelor in Andonia post-WWII. He saw the waning sales at the Hotel Jeanne D'Arc and invested in it, even taking a penthouse suite to call his home. He also gifted the hotel the famous taxidermied bear, which is often mistaken as a grizzly. The bear is, in fact, a polar bear dyed brown, and it is of Russian origin but had made its way to a Nazi mansion, and was later stolen by Frank Howell's squadron and shipped back to Illinois.

Frank Howell remained a bachelor for the rest of his life, though rumors existed of his strange sexual proclivity that involved BDSM and young girls.

In 1968 Frank Howell was found hanged in his penthouse in the Hotel Jeanne D'Arc. He was fifty-three years old. It was presumed suicide, though many doubted this and assumed it was an accident of auto-erotic asphyxiation.

He is interred at St. Anthony's Garden Cemetery. A stone re-creation of the taxidermied bear stands guard at his tomb.

20.

Chris's Third Nipple

Driving past St. Anthony's Garden Cemetery, Chris holds his breath and knocks on the window. An old superstition. Something he learned from his sister when he was a kid. Hold your breath so the spirits don't enter. Knock the glass to scare them away. Now it's just a habit, something he can't help but do every time he passes St. Anthony's and its weird gate and old tombstones.

"Yes?" Lily has her seatback down. She said it was to stretch her back, but she's reached over and her hand is on Chris's thigh. "You knocked?"

"We're here," he says. He pulls past the orange sign of the Popeyes, pulls into his parking lot.

"Nice pond," Lily says.

In his apartment, she asks if he has anything to drink. He offers her water, says, "I could shave some barbiturates into it if you like." He doesn't even know if he's joking anymore.

She sits on the couch and takes off her shirt. She's not wearing a bra. He's seeing the breasts he held earlier, and his heart rate increases again. Maybe the methylphenidate. Maybe the three-story walk up. Maybe lust. Maybe love.

"Want to smoke?" He points to the bowl on the coffee table next to the book about Illinois cults.

"Get naked," she says.

Chris obeys, stripping off his fleece, his chinos. He's wearing white briefs today and he prays there are no skid marks as he pulls them down. He keeps his T-shirt on, but she doesn't seem to care. She wants to see his ass, and he worries again about the hygiene of it all.

"No tail," she says.

"No, no tail." He laughs. She's an oddball, Chris, but so pretty. *Impress* her. "I have a third nipple though."

He takes off his shirt. He is round and hairy and very, very white. Beneath his left nipple, a few inches down, is a pink circle, an areola, an unformed nipple.

"My mom calls it my witch's mark," he says.

"Your mother was a witch?" she says. "I knew it."

Lily is quickly kissing his third nipple. She's licking it. What the hell is going on? Chris, this beautiful girl is maybe a little wild.

He pulls her up, kisses her neck, her earlobe, her cheek. His lips meet hers and they're making out, but her hands are on the small of his back creeping to the top of his ass crack. She's rubbing him, like a bad massage, and he maneuvers out of her grip, lies down on the couch and says, dumbly, "C'mere."

She slips off her jeans and crawls on top of him, but despite his heart rate, despite his lust, despite what he's feeling, he's flaccid. He tries. He tugs. He closes his eyes to focus, and tugs some more. It's the weed. It's the drugs. It's the caffeine. It's the stress. It's what Dr. Grenman said. Damn, now he just sees Dr. Grenman and her pearl necklace.

"I'm sorry," he says. He offers to go down on her, but she reaches for her pants.

"Another time," she says. "We'll do this right, another time."

"Do you want to stay," he says. "Hang out?"

She's looking past him, she's done. He can see it. He can see she won't see him again. Will he be able to go to the only decent coffee shop in town anymore? Will he have to get coffee from Aloha Jim now?

"It's getting late," she says. "My sister is probably worried."

"Okay," he says. "I can drive you home."

She wants to get laid, but she knows she should sober up. She's too much of a lightweight now, and after two glasses of wine and a martini, she is too drunk. Or maybe he shaved barbiturates into her drink? It seems unlikely. No, Lily watched him. Plus, he seems too timid to try that. He's sweet, actually. She did wish he had a tail, though.

Outside Chris's apartment, an old man in cowboy gear is holding up a bag of what looks like feces. He's lit by the full moon and the Popeyes sign. The man asks if Lily is a doctor too.

"No," she says. "Why? Are you a doctor?"

Chris is inside, pissing. Or as he put it, *tinkling*.

"No," the man says. "You the doctor's girlfriend?"

"What is that?" She points at the bag.

"My insides are falling out of me," the man says. "My insides are seeping out every time I sit down to do my duty. I fear this is my liver."

Lily looks at the bag of shit, then at the man, his long legs in bootcut jeans, the belt buckle with a rodeo cowboy riding a bull. He wears turquoise jewelry, has turquoise eyes.

"Have you tried dancing?" she asks.

"I'm sorry?"

"You should try dancing," she says. "You've got the gams for it. And it keeps your organs inside you."

21.
Lily Meets Harvey

She can be cruel when she's drunk, and she scoffs when the man drops his bag.

"Hey, Harv," Chris says, grabbing Lily's hand and closing the door behind him. "This is Lily."

"She thinks I should dance for my organs," Harv says.

"You've been drinking, Harv," Chris says.

"Maybe."

"How are you supposed to sleep with the drink in you," Chris mock-scolds the old neighbor. "Let me see that bag."

Lily watches Chris examine the sandwich bag, to her surprise. He has taken on an air of confidence she has yet to see—the big man inside matches the outside.

"I think today is a good day, Harv."

"How's that?"

"Your organs aren't in here," Chris says. "Now I got to drive the lady home."

He leans toward Lily, whispers in her ear, "I'll wash my hands first."

Lily is left alone again on the landing with the old neighbor. He looks her up and down, but she detects no animus and no desire. He's fidgeting with his jewelry, his belt buckle. Finally he says, "He a good lay?"

"The best," Lily says. "Cock like a Titan. A total tripod."

The old man blushes.

"You ever have a giant cock in you?" Lily asks, and before he can answer, Chris is back outside and the old man is slinking away with his bag of shit.

22.
Harvey's Secret, Part II

The man Harvey Mulligan killed in a fight outside of Smith Street Bar on what is now Jimmy Suggs Road was Alvin Suggs, cousin to Jimmy Suggs, interred in the same tomb as the comedian, the comedian's father, and Alvin Suggs's father. Harvey Mulligan and Alvin Suggs had been lovers, and the fatal fight outside of Smith Street Bar was a lovers' quarrel, according to the police report. According to Harvey's own testimony, Alvin wanted to come out of the closet, and wanted Harvey to, as well. Alvin wanted them to move to Chicago and start a life together. The judge noted the irony of Harvey's testimony effectively acting as the coming-out his lover had wanted. At his parole hearing, Harvey had claimed he was born-again as a heterosexual Christian man, and noted that his fight was when he was lost in sin, and he had accidentally killed a man he should've saved, "a man who was trying to drag him to Hell on Earth," but he feared Alvin and his power.

The "gay panic" defense worked in the parole board hearing and Harvey Mulligan only served four years of his fifteen-year sentence.

23.

In the Heart in the Heart of the Country

Lily lives on a tree-lined block in Andonia Heights, the expensive neighborhood where Chris's professors live. Chris is almost certain Dr. Grenman lives on this block. He went there for a Christmas party last year. And this is the neighborhood where the gay corrupt congressman lives, the one who is getting censured. He bought his house here mysteriously for $200,000 under market value, Chris had seen on the news.

Chris is still parked around the corner from Lily's house. He dropped her off five, ten minutes earlier, but he needs a rest. His engine and lights are off, but he can see his hand shaking by the bright moonlight. He needs to examine the day, examine, if he can, a conquest and a failure, and he needs to think about what Dr. Grenman is going to say to a disciplinary committee.

Would it be in Chris's favor (or against it) if they knew the GTA asked him out on a date after the exam? He could say it showed his excellent bedside manner, haha, if you know what I mean, haha.

Yikes, Chris, take another Ritalin, you're delirious. Maybe you should take a Klonopin to ease the stress, but you don't have any in the car, do you? Check the glove compartment. No. Another Ritalin it is. Anyway, it should help you drive home.

Whoo-boy, Chris, you're feeling that, the blood rush, the head clear, and the heart race. It's beating a million miles a minute, but you know that's not physically possible, you know what's happening. The pain is shooting through your chest, Chris. Is there pain in your arm? Is this a heart attack? Get out of the car. Get out of the car, remember where Dr. Grenman lives, right there, yes, get to her door and ring the bell. Chris, her house is there, get to it, get to the bell, get there, get there, get there, you're going to be all right.

24.
Landing in Andonia

Lily's nephew is already asleep when she gets home, and her sister is watching TV.

"You've got to see this," her sister says.

"What?" Lily comes into the living room, sits on the floor by Alistair's trains, and leans against the couch.

"I was watching the news and they had one of those 'Will It Land in Andonia?' segments so I DVR'd it. This one was filmed right outside Fifty-Fifty. I can see you in the coffee shop."

Lily watches the screen, watches a newsman in a gray suit interviewing the blue-haired woman with the slutty-cat sweatshirt. *Take a picture, it'll last longer.*

25.

The Five-Second Rule Stands in Andonia

Interviewer: I'm standing here outside of Fifty-Fifty coffee shop in Andonia, Illinois, speaking with—

Woman: Meredith Mulligan.

Interviewer: Meredith, your local congressman is mired in controversy. He's been seen hobnobbing with gay men in Provincetown. He decorated his congressional office—at the taxpayer's cost—to look like a Hogwarts house. Hufflepuff! And it's rumored that he has been having an affair with a staffer. A *male* staffer. Meredith, how does this land in Andonia?

Woman: Well, corruption's what happens when people are in power.

Interviewer: And you're okay with that?

Woman: I'm not going to vote for him if he runs again, if that's what you're asking.

Interviewer: Excellent, now I'd like to ask your opinion on some of the larger-scope things happening. Congress has recently reacted to the scandals of sexual assault accusations rocking Washington, Wall Street, and Hollywood. Today, famed television star Cory Rupter has been accused of taking lewd photographs of young Latino men on his yacht. Now a congressman from Texas, from the district where Rupter owns what some are calling "a private sex ranch," has asked on the congressional floor for stricter policy against young men crossing the border and entering Texas, saying if these young Latino men aren't in Texas they won't be photographed. There's also a rumor Rupter will run for president. How does this land in Andonia?

Woman: Oh, that's nothing.

Interviewer: What is nothing?

Woman: Taking pictures. I had much worse done to me.

Interviewer: I'm sorry?

Woman: For starters, I was once raped in a graveyard.

Interviewer: I am sorry, was this…. When was this?

Woman: Oh, I don't know. I was thirteen. The man was in his forties.

Interviewer: And is this the first time you're telling your story?

Woman: I told friends, and I told my brother, but that was so long ago.

Interviewer: Is the man who did this to you, did you know him?

Woman: Everyone knew him. He was Frank Howell, the playboy of Andonia and heir to the Howell fortune.

Interviewer: As in Howell Industries?

Woman: Yes.

Woman shrugs and looks around, as if to say, All of this. *She waves her donut in the air.*

Interviewer: And you said in a graveyard?

Woman: St. Anthony's. He wanted to have sex on his father's grave. I met him working at the Hotel Jeanne D'Arc, cleaning rooms. He had a penthouse, and he told me he wanted to give me an extra job to do. I asked what it was, and he said, "Clean my father's grave." I told him that I was scared to do that, and he offered me a lot of money.

Interviewer: How much?

Woman: I was a thirteen-year-old girl whose big brother was about to go to prison, and we needed help paying for a lawyer.

Interviewer: I see.

Woman: So whatever was offered felt like a lot. Maybe it was a hundred bucks.

Interviewer: And Frank Howell, heir to Howell Industries, took you to the cemetery?

Woman: St. Anthony's, yes.

Interviewer: And he raped you.

Woman: And he raped me, yes. But back then we just called it "a bad date."

A large man walks into the frame, knocks the donut from the woman's hand, apologizes, and disappears again on the other side of the frame. The woman bends down, picks up the donut off the ground, and takes a bite.

26.
Chris's Ghost

When Chris returns, Harvey is waiting outside his door again.

Three hours have passed since Chris left to take Lily home. He dropped her off then spent hours on Dr. Grenman's couch. It was a panic attack, not a heart attack. Dr. Grenman is going to let Chris take a medical leave of absence for the rest of the semester. She said she could get him into a rehab facility outside Nauvoo. She told him what to pack, and to meet her back at her place in the morning. A medical leave of absence from a medical school.

Chris approaches his floor. He is tired of the game with the old man. Before Harvey can speak, Chris says, "Harvey? There's nothing more the bags can tell me."

"What about my diseases?" the old man asks.

Why is this man haunting him? Chris thinks about Lily, about her friend Silvia and the apparition in the grocery store. Schizotypal disorder, maybe? Pretty crazy. Pretty and crazy. And then there's Chris.

He's not pretty, definitely crazy. Definitely an addict. A panic attack? It was the Ritalin. It was the ED. It was the ghost story. It was Dr. Grenman. It was his dad and his heart-surgeon uncle. Dr. Grenman is right. It was the cocktail of drugs.

"My diseases, Doc?" Harvey snaps.

Chris sighs. "You're depressed."

"Depressed?"

"It's a real problem," Chris says. "Fucking depression, Harv."

"That's it?" Harvey says, angry.

"Well," Chris says. "You're also an alcoholic."

"No I'm not," the old man spits. "I'm no drunk and I ain't depressed."

"You're from here, right? Andonia born and raised?"

"Yeah," he says.

"This town is fucking depressing." Chris looks down at the pond. The full moon and the Popeyes sign reflect off its half-frozen surface. For the first time ever, it looks oddly serene. Still, Chris can smell the sewage emanating from it. "It's the fucking pits. It's a cursed hellhole. Look at this muddy pond. The orange glare from the Popeyes. Smell the air. Do you smell that? It smells like shit, and not just the shit you have in your bag. How can you *not* be depressed?"

Harvey is about to object, but Chris stops him with a half-raised hand.

"You're lonely, and you're sad, and you drink and maybe do some drugs, and it makes you sadder," Chris says. "You don't know who you are or what you want. You don't even know where you are."

"Of course I know where I am," Harvey says. "I'm at home in Andonia."

"You dress like this is Arizona, Harv, what the fuck is that about? It's fucking weird, you're weird. You're a sad, depressed drunk."

"No, I'm not sad. You're the sad one, fatty! You're the lonely one, fat ass! You're always alone, you're always moping, you're always sad. You're fat and sad, fatty!"

There is no arguing with a broken clock or an old drunk, so Chris, unable to articulate what has eaten away at him in this awful place, screams. His scream is ancient, prehistoric. It is the scream of a Neanderthal outside the gates of Eden. He looks up at the moon, at the Popeyes sign even, and he screams some more. He screams a loud, guttural scream, the kind of scream meant to release demons, anxieties, ghosts. He screams like Adam never took a bite of the apple and men are nothing more than wild animals. His scream will change the course of time, it'll change Chris's destiny, it'll shake this fucking town to the ground.

But the scream only garners Chris the ire of neighbors, the calls of "shut the fuck up" from other floors. The scream scatters annoyed birds flying off trees, and when the scream is done, Harvey opens his sandwich baggie, scoops his hand in, and launches his cold shit at Chris's face. Then the old man starts laughing. Harvey is bent over, struggling for breath he's laughing so hard.

The old man continues to laugh at Chris, to laugh at the fat-and-angry man covered in shit, but Chris turns, walks into his apartment, and closes the door behind him. Chris listens as his neighbor stomps back into his apartment. The walls are so thin he can hear the ice clink in the glass when Harvey has finally had his last laugh. Seconds pass, and he listens to the sound of Harvey's mutterings, the return of the raspy laugh. Chris washes his face and neck and hands in the kitchen sink, takes his shirt and pants off and throws them in the trash. He is stripped to his underwear, wet, and somewhat soapy. He goes to the closet, pulls out a suitcase to pack for tomorrow. What does he pack to go to rehab? He should probably flush his pills, right?

He hears Harvey again. Old man is crying now.

Chris turns on the TV, turns up the volume, flips to the news channel, and recognizes the segment immediately. It must be the fifth time they've played it today. A woman is being interviewed outside Fifty-Fifty, the reporter is asking a slew of questions about how to "fix" America. She starts talking about her sexual assault, and they're interrupted by Chris, his fat body knocking through the frame. The interviewer in the gray suit stifles a laugh, his false compassion for the old woman gone as soon as Chris stumbles into sight and fumbles the woman's donut.

Acknowledgments

Landing in Andonia started as a 4,000-word short story that I brought to my first MFA workshop at Columbia. The novelette is inspired by the months I lived with my sister, Caroline, and my nephew, Sebastian. I was able to write about medical school and medications because I took my friend (now Dr.) Madeleine Lipshie-Williams out to lunch before writing the first draft. I continued to bring edits of this project to workshops; I am grateful to have had Jean Kyoung Frazier and Franz Nicolay in both my second-year grad-school workshops, and we were extremely fortunate to have Sam Lipsyte as our theses advisor.

After Columbia I expanded this story while at the Catwalk Art Residency in Catskill, New York, and I continued to work on it in the quiet of the Institute Library in New Haven, Connecticut. Over the years, I've had several regular readers of my work who I'd like to thank for their input: Myles Ehrlich, Jackie LaSorda, and CC Perry; and more recently, Sola Saar, Shelby Wardlaw, and Theresa Lin. This story has tripled in length since its first draft, making it awkwardly long for a typical literary journal to publish but too short to pitch as a novella. Thus, I am deeply appreciative of *CRAFT* for hosting this novelette contest, Hanna Pylväinen for selecting *Landing in Andonia* as the contest's winner, and Courtney Harler along with the editorial teams at *CRAFT*, Discover New Art, and Red Mare Press for publishing my novelette as its own little book. I would like to thank, additionally, my Illinois-born-and-raised parents, as well as Anna, Caitlin, Dena, Peter, and Krystle.

But mostly, I must acknowledge my husband for his patience, love, and support. Thank you, Rory Hamovit, for being the best person in the world.

www.ingramcontent.com/pod-product-compliance
Lightning Source LLC
Chambersburg PA
CBHW070344010826
48976CB00019B/2614